In the Rain
with
Baby Duck

Amy Hest

illustrated by **Jill Barton**

CANDLEWICK PRESS
CAMBRIDGE, MASSACHUSETTS

P

it-pat.

Pit-a-pat.

Pit-a-pit-a-pat.

Oh, the rain came down.

It poured and poured.

Baby Duck was mad.

She did not like walking in the rain.

But it was Pancake Sunday, a Duck family

tradition, and Baby loved pancakes.

And she loved Grampa, who was waiting

on the other side of town.

For Lon, who loves umbrellas,
and for Ivy and Ian, the Florida cousins

A. H.

For Natalie and Sophie Lou,
my granddaughters

J. B.

Text copyright © 1995 by Amy Hest
Illustrations copyright © 1995 by Jill Barton

All rights reserved.

First edition 1995

Library of Congress Cataloging-in-Publication Data

Hest, Amy.
In the rain with Baby Duck / Amy Hest : illustrated by Jill Barton.—1st ed.
Summary: Although her parents love walking in the rain, Baby Duck does
not—until Grampa shares a secret with her.
ISBN 1-56402-532-2
[1. Rain and rainfall—Fiction. 2. Ducks—Fiction.
3. Grandfathers—Fiction.] I. Barton, Jill, ill. II. Title.
PZ7.H4375In   1995
[E]—dc20   94-48929
4 6 8 10 9 7 5

Printed in Hong Kong

This book was typeset in Opti Lucius Ad Bold.
The pictures were done in pencil and watercolor.

Candlewick Press
2067 Massachusetts Avenue
Cambridge, Massachusetts 02140

Pit-pat. Pit-a-pat. Pit-a-pit-a-pat.

"Follow us! Step lively!" Mr. and Mrs.

Duck left the house arm in arm.

"Wet feet," wailed Baby.

"Don't dally, dear.

Don't drag behind,"

called Mr. Duck.

"Wet face," pouted Baby. "Water in my eyes."

Mrs. Duck pranced along. "See how
the rain rolls off your back!"

"Mud," muttered Baby.

"Mud, mud, mud."

"Don't dawdle, dear! Don't lag behind!"

Mr. and Mrs. Duck skipped ahead.

They waddled. They shimmied.

They hopped in all the puddles.

Baby dawdled. She dallied and

pouted and dragged behind.

She sang a little song.

"I do not like the rain one bit

Splashing down my neck.

Baby feathers soaking wet,

I do not like this mean old day."

"Are you singing?" called Mr. and Mrs. Duck.

"What a fine thing to do in the rain!"

Baby stopped singing.

Grampa was waiting at the front door.

He put his arm around Baby.

"Wet feet?" he asked.

"Yes," Baby said.

"Wet face?"

Grampa asked.

"Yes," Baby said.

"Mud?" Grampa asked.

"Yes," Baby said. "Mud, mud, mud."

"I'm afraid the rain makes Baby cranky,"
  clucked Mr. Duck.

"I've never heard of a duck who doesn't
  like rain," worried Mrs. Duck.

"Is that a fact?" Grampa kissed Baby's cheeks.

Grampa took Baby's hand.

"Come with me, Baby."

They went upstairs to the attic.

"We are looking for a tall, green bag," Grampa said.

Finally they found it.

Inside was a beautiful red umbrella.

There were matching boots, too.

"These used to be your mother's," Grampa whispered. "A long time ago, she was a baby duck who did not like rain."

Baby opened the umbrella.

The boots were just the right size.

Baby and Grampa marched downstairs.

"My boots!" cried Mrs. Duck. "And my bunny umbrella!"

"No, mine!" said Baby.

"You look lovely," said Mrs. Duck.

Mr. Duck put a platter of pancakes on the table.

After that, Baby and Grampa went outside.

Pit-pat. Pit-a-pat. Pit-a-pit-a-pat.

Oh, the rain came down.

It poured and poured.

Baby Duck and Grampa

walked arm in arm

in the rain.

They
waddled.

They
shimmied.

They hopped in all
the puddles.

And Baby Duck sang a new song.

"I really like the rain a lot
Splashing my umbrella.
Big red boots on baby feet,
I really love this rainy day."